Where Is My Gift From God?

HANNAH KUCERA

AuthorHouse™
1663 Liberty Drive
Bloomington, IN 47403
www.authorhouse.com
Phone: 833-262-8899

Because of the dynamic nature of the Internet, any web addresses or links contained in this book may have changed since publication and may no longer be valid. The views expressed in this work are solely those of the author and do not necessarily reflect the views of the publisher, and the publisher hereby disclaims any responsibility for them.

Any people depicted in stock imagery provided by Getty Images are models, and such images are being used for illustrative purposes only.
Certain stock imagery © Getty Images.

This book is printed on acid-free paper.

ISBN: 979-8-8230-4187-4 (sc)
ISBN: 979-8-8230-4188-1 (e)

Library of Congress Control Number: 2025900529

Print information available on the last page.

Published by AuthorHouse 01/24/2025

authorHOUSE®

To my mom and dad, who showed me what it looks like to
use the gifts God gives you for the good of others.

To the readers of this book, young and young at heart, may this book
remind you that the uniqueness you are yearning for is already yours.

Hannah and her mom were gazing up at the stars when a rush of questions came flying out of Hannah's mouth... "Mom, what makes the stars shine so bright?" How do cheetahs run so fast? How can cowgirls ride a horse? And where did eagles learn how to fly?

Hannah's mom replied, "Those are their gifts. God gives everyone a gift which makes us all unique."

Hannah began to wonder, where is my gift from God?

Hannah set out on a mission to find her gift from God. She searched far and wide, high and low for this gift everyone else seemed to have...

3

She traveled through the deserts in
Texas, looking around cacti and under
armadillos...but found nothing.

She traveled through the streets of New York, hailing taxis left and right but not a single one carried a gift from God.

TAXI!!

TAXI-03

5

She even drove a boat across the ocean,
finding lots of fish, but not a single gift
wrapped with ribbon or a bow.

Hannah became discouraged. She cried
to her mom, "I have looked everywhere
and I can't find my gift from God!"

Hannah's mom replied, "Oh Hannah, your gift from God isn't something that will show up in a box or wrapped with ribbon. Your gifts are already inside of you. Think about all of your talents. Talents are the things you are good at...

Hannah said "hmm, I think I understand what gifts from God are now! Tomorrow, I will discover which ones God gave ME!"

The next day Hannah set out to
find what she was good at...

She tried running with the cheetahs...

but simply could not keep up.

She attempted to fly like the birds in the sky...

but could barely get her feet off the ground.

She even tried to ride a
horse at the rodeo but
had no luck there either.

Hannah came back to her mom in tears, "I've tried everything but I can't run like a cheetah, soar like an eagle, or ride a horse like a cowgirl!"

"That's because you are looking for someone else's gift, Hannah's mom exclaimed. "God made you wonderfully unique with many gifts so you can share them with the world!"

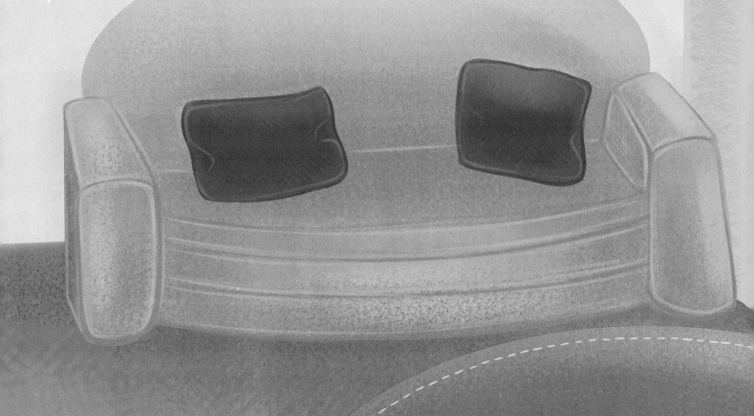

He gave you a cheerful spirit
to share with others.

He gave you your smile to turn
others' frowns upside down.

He gave you a uniquely determined
brain so you never give up.

He gave you a heart that is filled
with faith. And so much more!

Hannah exclaimed, "You're right, God really did give me gifts! And now I know that He gave everyone a special gift!"

My sister is brave and uses that gift to calm me down when I am feeling fearful. My brother is witty and always makes me laugh.

My dad is hard working and uses that gift to help others.

My friend Kate is understanding and tender hearted which makes her a great listener.

"And God gave you gifts too, mom!
He made you patient and thoughtful.
You were able to help me see my
gifts no matter how long it took!"

God gave me many gifts and
he gave YOU gifts too!"

What gifts do you have?

Gratitude

Big smile

Hopeful spirit

Kind heart

Contagious laugh

Positivity

Thoughtfulness

Determination

Modesty

Selflessness

Honesty

Patience

Compassion

Hannah experienced various trials and tribulations before she would discover her gifts from God. She would search in all the wrong places looking for validation by going on various adventures throughout the world. Hannah learns that while physical attributes and worldly knowledge can be important, they do not compare to the positive effect our God-given gifts can have on others. The purpose of this book is to inspire confidence in children of all ages and abilities so they always know the importance of their uniqueness.